PICKLE

Poppy Pickle lived in an ordinary house with an ordinary dad, an ordinary mum and three ordinary cats...

But Poppy Pickle was not ordinary. Far from it.

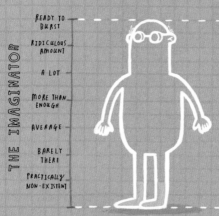

You see, Poppy Pickle was full to the brim with imagination.

Sometimes Poppy's imagination got her into a bit of a pickle.

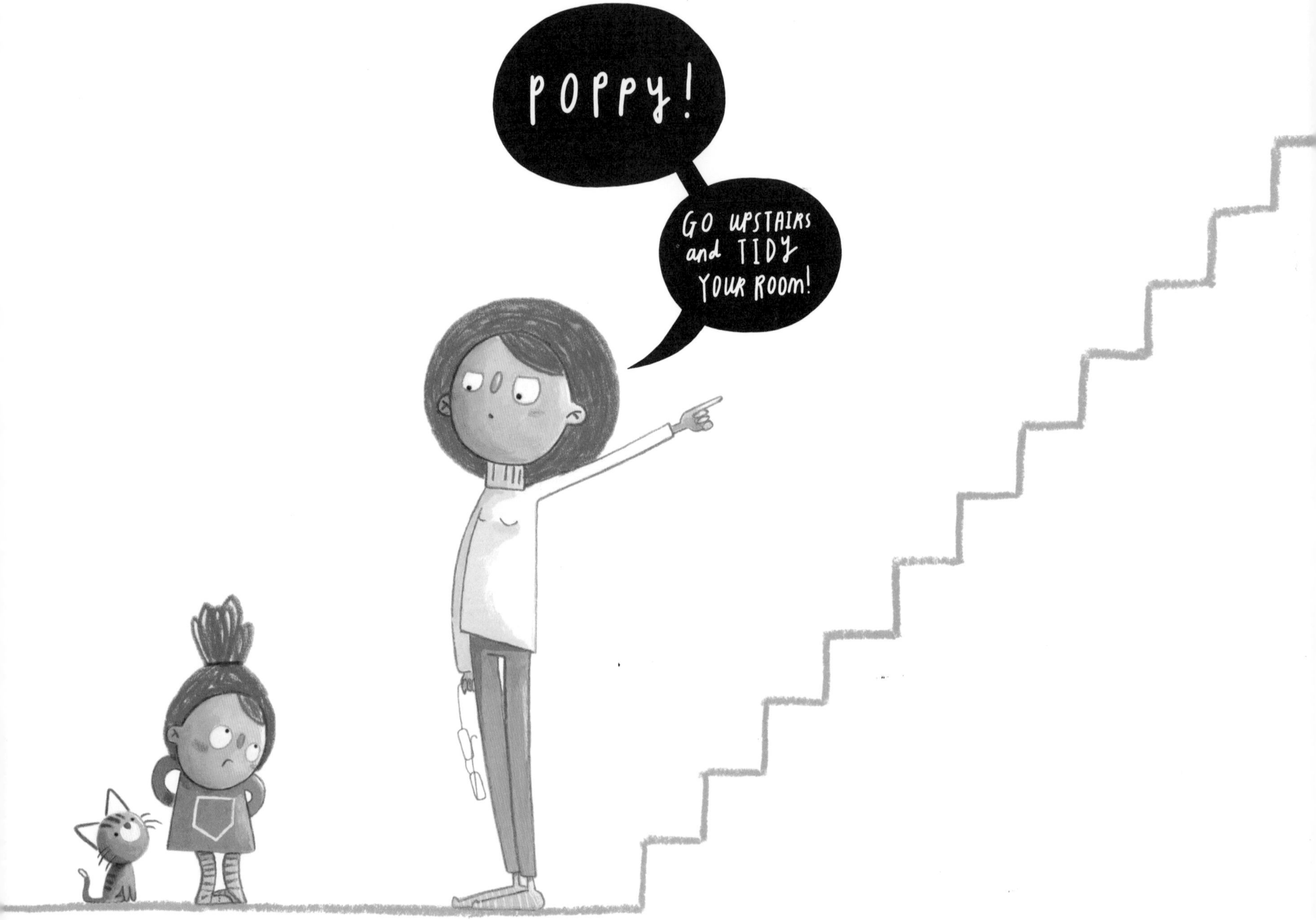
POPPY!
GO UPSTAIRS and TIDY YOUR ROOM!

Poppy went upstairs,
but she didn't tidy her room.

Instead
she started
imagining…

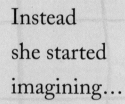

And suddenly the strangest
thing happened.

POP!

Her imagination came…

ALIVE!

It was incredible.
It was amazing.
It was **magic**.

Soon Poppy was imagining
all kinds of things!

Poppy
imagined
big.

POP!

Poppy imagined small.

Poppy imagined far and inbetween
and back to front and upside down.

Never-ending POCKET MONEY

A CASTLE made of CAKE

A CHOCOLATE TREE

Poppy Pickle imagined it **all**.

A Talking GOLDEN GOLDFISH

OH HEY!

A GHOST

A SPACE ROCKET

A Baby T-REX

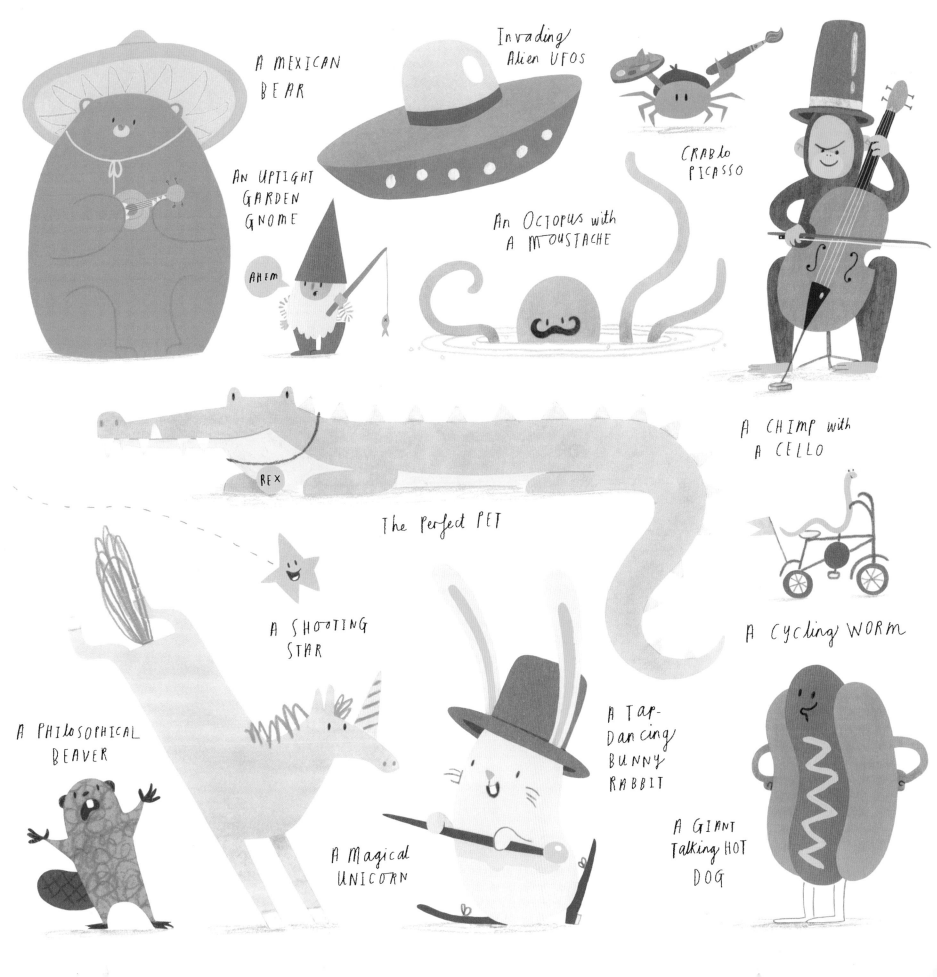

A MEXICAN BEAR

Invading Alien UFOS

CRABlo PICASSO

AN UPTIGHT GARDEN GNOME

AHEM

An OCTOPUS with A MOUSTACHE

A CHIMP with A CELLO

REX

The Perfect PET

A SHOOTING STAR

A Cycling WORM

A PHILOSOPHICAL BEAVER

A Magical UNICORN

A Tap-Dancing BUNNY RABBIT

A GIANT Talking HOT DOG

Soon Poppy's room was filled with
weird and wonderful creatures.

Poppy was having the time of her life.
Until...

...it all started to go **very,**

very

wrong.

And then everything went from very wrong to totally terrible!

Poppy was in a **huge** pickle!

She had to get rid of everything FAST – before Mum and Dad found out!

Un-imagining the creatures didn't work... at... all!

So Poppy imagined a giant eraser to rub them out. But imaginary creatures are very tricky to catch, and Poppy was running out of time. Mum and Dad were at the door.

Quick as a flash,
a **door** appeared.

It was hard work pushing everyone through...

But Poppy did it.

Just in time...

It took Poppy **all** afternoon to clear up the mess.
When she had finally finished it was dinner time...

and she was still in trouble.

Big trouble.

PUFF